D1275521

For Max

Also published by Ruwanga Trading:

The Goodnight Gecko
The Whale Who Wanted to be Small
The Wonderful Journey
A Whale's Tale
The Gift of Aloha
The Shark Who Learned a Lesson
Gecko Hide and Seek
The Brave Little Turtle
Tikki Turtle's Quest
Happy as a Dolphin, *A Child's Celebration of Hawai'i*
The Pink Parrot *(available as an e-book)*
How the Geckos Learned to Chirp

For more information and fun activities, visit Gill's website:
www.HawaiianChildrensBooks.com

First published 2014 by Ruwanga Trading
ISBN 978-0-9701528-4-8
Printed in China by Everbest Printing Co., Ltd

© 2014 Gill McBarnet

BOOK ENQUIRIES AND ORDERS:
Booklines Hawaii, a division of The Islander Group
269 Pali'i Street
Mililani, Hawaii 96789
Phone: 808-676-0116, ext.206
Fax: 808-676-5156
Toll Free: 1-877-828-4852
Website: www.islandergroup.com

The Rainbow Mermaids of Hawaii

Written and illustrated by Gill McBarnet

One Rainbow mermaid

with tail of shimmering blue,

Is joined by her sister

so now there are Two.

Two Rainbow mermaids
see the fishes flee,

Three dreamy mermaids
wishing there were more,

When – SWISH SWISH their wish comes true as now there are Four.

Four frolicking mermaids
jumping in the waves.
Each does a daring dive,
and now there are Five.

Doing some amazing tricks,
and suddenly – there are Six!

Along comes another,
so now there are Seven.

Seven sleek mermaids
slipping through the sea -

One joins them at the gate,

so now there are Eight.

Eight friendly mermaids
cruise behind canoes -
Having such a carefree time,
and now there are Nine.

Ten twirling mermaids
heading back to shore ...
Surfing all the curling waves,
then going back for more!

The Ten rainbow mermaids
could play like this all day -
But suddenly they remember
what day it is today

They have a date with birthday cake
and really can't be late!
...for One Rainbow Mermaid
with tail of shimmering blue,
surrounded by her Rainbow friends
in every color, too.